BERNARD WABER

Lyle
at the
Office

Houghton Mifflin Company Boston

for my granddaughter

Anna

For information about this and other Houghton Mifflin trade and reference books and multimedia products, visit The Bookstore at Houghton Mifflin on the World Wide Web at http://www.hmco.com/trade/.

Library of Congress Cataloging-in-Publication Data

Waber, Bernard
  Lyle at the office / Bernard Waber.
    p.   cm.
    Summary: When Lyle the crocodile visits Mr. Primm's advertising office, he is almost recruited as the Krispie Krunchie Krackles cereal spokesperson.
    ISBN 0-395-70563-0   PAP ISBN 0-395-82743-4
    [1. Crocodiles — Fiction. 2. Work — Fiction.]   I. Title.
PZ7.W113Lwe   1994   94-49644
[E] — dc20   CIP
                          AC

Printed in the United States of America
WOZ 10 9 8 7 6 5

Everybody thought Lyle the Crocodile
was funny—not silly funny,
or funny looking,
just plain funny.

And wherever he went,
Lyle always made people smile
and forget their troubles.

At the supermarket,
shoppers perked up
the instant they saw Lyle.

"We should offer Lyle a job,"
said the store's manager.
"Then we could always count
on having happy customers."

In the park, frowns turned to big, big smiles,
the minute Lyle appeared—
especially when he performed his tricks.

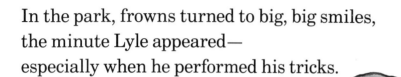

"Do you suppose Lyle would consider working
for us?" asked the parks commissioner.
"Our parks can use more cheer these days."

PARKS DEPT.

And once, a man wanted
to use a smiling picture of Lyle
in a toothpaste advertisement.
"Listen to this," said the man.
"'Smile like Lyle.'
Now, isn't that catchy!"

"No, thank you," the Primms always
answered, politely but firmly.
"Lyle is happy with his life just as it is."

Lyle was happy, all right,
living with Mr. and Mrs. Primm,
their children, Joshua and Miranda,
and his dear mother, Felicity—
or Nurse Felicity, as she was
known at the hospital where she worked.

Lyle loved to entertain
the family,
as he did one night
parading about
in the pirate costume
he would soon be wearing
on Halloween.

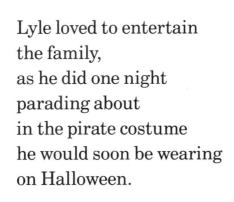

It was a joyful house made even more joyful by the arrival of the baby, Miranda.

Lyle adored showing off pictures of Miranda.

And he almost burst with pride
and did three somersaults
when his name was among the first words
Miranda learned to say.
"Ly—le! Ly—le!"
she would coo to him.

Yes, it was a good life,
especially for a crocodile.

And good things were always happening.
One day Mr. Primm took Lyle along for
a visit to his office.
Mr. Primm knew how eager Lyle was to visit,
and how much everyone at the office
wanted to meet Lyle.

Lyle gleefully waved goodbye
as the two set off for work.

As usual, morning traffic was heavy.

After much beeping and honking,
Mr. Primm and Lyle finally arrived at
the office building.

It was fun going through the revolving doors.
Lyle went round and round and round.

He loved pressing the elevator button.

Up, up, up they went.

Everyone in the office was so happy to see Lyle.

Lyle quickly made himself useful . . .
sharpening pencils . . .

delivering memos . . .

and operating the copying machine.

He made so many friends.
They all commented on his good manners.

Lyle even sat in on a
very important meeting.

He enjoyed an excellent lunch,
and delightful company,
in the office cafeteria.
Lyle had two slices of pizza
and an orange drink.

Best of all, Lyle visited the company's day-care center.

He spent much of the day
joyfully playing with and amusing
the children.

But when it was time to say goodbye,
the children cried, "We want to stay with Lyle."
"Please, Lyle, promise to come back,"
said some of the parents.

Sadly, Lyle waved goodbye to the children
and returned to Mr. Primm's room.

Mr. Primm was busy trying to think
up new ideas for Krispie Krunchie Krackles cereal.
That was Mr. Primm's job, thinking up ideas.
But at the moment Mr. Primm had
no ideas whatsoever—absolutely none.

Feeling rather empty, Mr. Primm
shared a sample box of
Krispie Krunchie Krackles with Lyle.

POP! CRUNCH! CRACKLE! CRACKLE! CRUNCH!
Although Lyle tried to be quiet about it, everyone
was startled by the loud popping, crunching, crackling
sounds he made chewing Krispie Krunchie Krackles.

POP! CRUNCH! CRACKLE! CRACKLE! CRUNCH!
Even Mr. Bigg, who was Mr. Primm's boss,
and a busy person at that, heard him chewing
all the way down the hall.
"Who is making that racket?" shouted Mr. Bigg.

Mr. Bigg quickly discovered it was Lyle
who was making the racket. He was so surprised.
"Does Lyle really like eating Krispie Krunchie Krackles?"
asked Mr. Bigg.
"Of course," said Mr. Primm. "Doesn't everybody?"

Suddenly Mr. Bigg's face lit up. It lit up the way it always
lit up whenever Mr. Bigg had a brainstorm.
"That's it! That's it!" said Mr. Bigg. "Our new slogan will be
'Everybody, but everybody, loves Krispie Krunchie Krackles.'
And we'll put Lyle's picture on the cereal box.
How's that for a terrific idea!" said Mr. Bigg.

"Oh, no," said Mr. Primm.

"Oh, yes," said Mr. Bigg.

"But you can't put Lyle's picture on
a cereal box," said Mr. Primm.

"And why not?" said Mr. Bigg.

"Because . . . well . . . Lyle is a very private crocodile."

"Nonsense, no such thing as private. I'll call the
photographers at once. This is dynamite," said Mr. Bigg.

"I can see it now," said Mr. Bigg. "Lyle smiling,
holding a bowl filled with delicious, nutritious
Krispie Krunchie Krackles in one hand,
a gleaming spoon in the other,
saying, 'Yum, Yum, Yummy Yum Yum,
oh, how I love my Krispie Krunchie Krackles.'"

"Lyle will never say, 'Yum, Yum, Yummy Yum, Yum,'"
said Mr. Primm, "nor will his picture be on
a cereal box."
"We'll discuss all that later," said Mr. Bigg,
dialing the photographers.

"We won't ever discuss it,"
said Mr. Primm,
walking out with Lyle.

"Where are you going with Lyle?"
called Mr. Bigg. "Primm, come back here!
Primm! Primm!
Sir! Consider yourself dismissed!"
a fuming Mr. Bigg shouted after them.
"And that goes for your crocodile, too,"
he added rather foolishly.

When the family heard about it,
Joshua thought it might have been really neat,
and great fun for kids, to have Lyle's picture on
thousands of cereal boxes.
But Mrs. Primm definitely agreed with Mr. Primm.
"No cereal boxes," she said.
"And no job," said Mr. Primm.
"We'll all do just fine, thank you," said Mrs. Primm.

And the family did do just fine.
Each soon found a way to earn money.
Joshua walked dogs.

Lyle took plant-sitting jobs.

Felicity put in extra hours at the hospital.
Mrs. Primm worked late into the night in
her home office. She wrote about new books
for a neighborhood newspaper.
And every day Mr. Primm looked for a new job.

Meanwhile, back at the office
everyone missed Mr. Primm
—even Mr. Bigg.
And the day-care center children
kept asking for Lyle.

More cheerfully, the family had so much
looked forward to Halloween,
and at long last the big night arrived.

Lyle finally got to wear his pirate costume.
Joshua dressed up as a monster,
and Miranda was an adorable little witch.
Mr. and Mrs. Primm and Felicity
accompanied them trick-or-treating.

"Trick-or-treat! Trick-or-treat!"
they called out as doors swung open
and their bags filled with Halloween goodies.

But there was one doorbell they dared not ring.
That bell belonged to the rundown,
gloomy house they were just passing.
"What a pity," said Mrs. Primm about the house.
"It's been empty for years," said Mr. Primm.
"That's because it's haunted," said Joshua.
"Everybody knows there are ghosts inside."
Ghosts! Lyle's eyes widened.

"And do you know what?" Joshua went on.
"Cries for help have been heard coming
from inside the house."
"Oh, Joshua," said Mrs. Primm.

POST
NO
BILLS

IVY

LOUIE
PAT

Mrs. Primm was about to add, "That's just gossip,"
when suddenly, in fact, they heard cries for help
coming from the house.
"What was that?" said Mr. Primm.
"Help! Help!"
"Those are real cries," said Mrs. Primm.

"Hello in there!" called Mr. Primm.
"Help! Help!" a voice called back.
Even though he was scared silly of ghosts,
Lyle pushed in the door only to discover . . .

MR. BIGG!
But what was Mr. Bigg up to now?
Well, at the moment, it seemed, he was busy
clinging for dear life to a ceiling light fixture.
"Help! Help!" cried Mr. Bigg. "My ladder
has fallen and I can't get down."

Lyle set the ladder upright and helped a very
shaken Mr. Bigg come down.
"Oh, Lyle, everyone, thank you, thank you,"
said Mr. Bigg. "You saved my life. I was here all alone,
putting light bulbs in this house,
which I will soon be moving into, when—"
"You are moving into this house!" they exclaimed.
Everyone was so surprised.

"Well . . . welcome! And good luck in your new
home," said Mr. Primm.
"Thank you," said Mr. Bigg.
And good luck with the ghosts! thought Lyle.

Day after day the family watched
Mr. Bigg's house being renovated.
Before long the old neglected house
was sparkly bright.
It looked so nice, Lyle began to wonder
if it was still haunted.

One day a letter from Mr. Bigg
arrived at the house on East 88th Street.
Mrs. Primm read it.

"Dear Primms,
and Dear Lyle and Felicity:

Please come to my housewarming party.
It's next Saturday afternoon at two."

And the letter was signed,

"Your new neighbor
(and friend, I hope),

Alwyn Power Bigg III

P.S. You can call me Al."

Everyone from the office came to the party—
and, most especially, the day-care center children.

"Please consider coming back to work,"
Mr. Bigg said to Mr. Primm. "We need you
—and miss you.
And . . . ahem . . . we'll just forget all about
having Lyle's picture on cereal boxes
—gem of an idea though it is.
Oh, and most important, we would certainly expect
many more visits to the office from Lyle."
Everyone smiled . . .

especially Lyle.